Published by Peter Haddock Ltd, Bridlington, England
© The Butterfly Children Limited
Created by Angela Mills and Pat Mills
Printed in India.

The Butterfly Children

NUTS AND LEAVES

CREATED BY ANGELA AND PAT MILLS
Story by Elisabeth Sackett
Illustrated by Angela Mills

ph

Deep in the woods, where people seldom go, live the Butterfly Children. Autumn had come and the leaves on the trees had turned to gold, red and orange. Everywhere the woods glowed with colour. Warm, brown nuts, dark purple and bright, red berries covered the bushes.

Chrissie was walking through the woods one bright morning. She wanted to find some rose-hips to make soothing syrup which was good for winter coughs and colds. The bushes were covered with white spiders' webs that sparkled in the sun. Chrissie was careful not to break them as she searched for berries. She was so busy she didn't hear DC coming until he shouted out right behind her, "'Morning Chrissie — what a great day!"

Chrissie jumped and dropped all the berries she had collected.

"Really, DC, what do you think you're doing? Can't you be more careful?"

"Sorry," said DC. "It's just so exciting in this weather! The wind is rising, I'm sure there will be a gale later on."

They both looked up into the sky and saw that the top branches of the trees were moving backwards and forwards making creaking noises while far above them the clouds were racing each other.

"Very interesting," snapped Chrissie. "Now will you please help me pick up all the berries I dropped."

"All right," said DC and together they gathered all the berries into Chrissie's basket.

"Let's see if we can find any juicy blackberries," said DC.

Chrissie agreed and they set off through the wood. They passed under an enormous oak tree.

"Oh!" cried Chrissie as something hard bounced off her head.

"Ouch!" shouted DC as something hard bounced off his head.

They looked up to where they heard a loud chattering noise coming from above them. A branch was shaking violently because a small red squirrel was jumping from one foot to the other and shrieking at the top of her voice. DC and Chrissie flew up to her.

"Whatever is the matter?" asked Chrissie. The squirrel shrieked louder than ever.

"Now just calm down," said DC severely, "and maybe we can help you. Tell us why you are so upset."

The squirrel stopped jumping and screamed, "Someone has stolen all the nuts I had stored for the winter and I won't have anything to eat until spring." She started sobbing quietly.

"Show us where you put your nuts. Then we will search in all the places nearby. Perhaps you have forgotten exactly where you put them," said Chrissie soothingly.

The squirrel sniffed. She was a very well-organised animal and knew exactly where her nuts should be. They all climbed down from the tree and started searching under the tree roots. The hole where the nuts had been was quite empty.

"See," said the squirrel, "no nuts."

The faint noise of shrieks and laughter came through the trees. Chrissie and DC looked at each other.

"It sounds like Red and Susie. Together those two mean trouble," said Chrissie.

"Come along!" cried DC. "Let's see what they are doing."

"Something they shouldn't be, I'm quite sure," said Chrissie as they flew off towards the noise.

As they got closer a loud thumping and clumping sound could be heard. The wind was blowing more strongly now and leaves were whirling down from the trees, but it couldn't be leaves making such a loud noise.

In a clearing in the trees they saw Red and Susie playing bowls. They were aiming at red and white toadstools and throwing hard, brown, shiny acorns. There was a large pile on the ground beside them and each acorn had a small mark on it. Red and Susie saw DC, Chrissie and the squirrel as they turned round to pick up more.

"I'm the best bowler!" cried Susie. "I've hit three toadstools !"

"No you're not!" said Red. "I've hit far more than that."

"Haven't!" shouted Susie. "You're a cheat. You can't count and you couldn't hit a chestnut tree if you were standing next to it!"

"You couldn't hit a chestnut tree if you were sitting on it!" Red shouted back.

"Be quiet!" said DC sternly as he walked towards them. "Where did you find these acorns?"

Red and Susie went rather red.

"Oh, they were just lying around," said Susie and looked away.

The squirrel ran over to the heap of acorns.

"They're mine!" she shrieked. "They've taken my acorns and they're damaging them!"

DC looked severely at Red and Susie. "Now, pick up all the acorns and put them back where you found them and find fresh ones to replace the ones you've damaged."

The two Butterfly Children sulkily started to collect the acorns together while the squirrel jumped and chattered behind them,

"Find me some new ones! I want lots of fat, tasty acorns in my store. I don't like bruised and dented ones!"

"I don't know why she wants all these acorns," Susie muttered, as she and Red searched among the tree roots.

"Squirrels need to keep stores of food for the winter. They get very hungry sometimes and they can't collect food when there's thick snow on the ground. You were both very thoughtless to steal her acorns," added Chrissie as Susie and Red put the acorns back into the hole under the tree roots. Then, exhausted by the hard work of gathering up all the acorns and storing them away, Susie and Red went back to their flowers.

DC and Chrissie left the squirrel counting the acorns and wandered off through the woods. The leaves swirled around them and they tried to catch them as they rushed past.

"You'll have a 'good-luck' day next year for every leaf you catch!" cried DC.

"I've just caught my first 'good-luck' day!" laughed Chrissie, as she snatched a golden-brown beech leaf from the air.

A mother deer and her fawn watched as the two Butterfly Children ran happily in the autumn sunshine.

A large chestnut leaf which had been torn off a tree by the wind passed them. As it whirled by they heard a voice shout, "This is wonderful! What a great ride! Leaf riding is the most exciting way to sp . . ."

The voice faded into the distance as the leaf sped away through the woods. Pete was standing on the leaf as it was blown through the air.

DC and Chrissie could just see Pete's face peering over the edge of the leaf. He was beginning to look rather worried. His two hands clung tightly to each side of the leaf. Then he disappeared from view.

"There's never any peace in these woods," moaned Chrissie. "I suppose we had better look for him."

As she and DC trudged off together in search of Pete, Chrissie told DC how many fruits needed to be picked to make cordials and preserves for the winter months.

"Sloes, blackberries and blueberries, hazelnuts." She began to count them off on her fingers. DC started to feel tired.

"Help!" cried a frightened voice from nearby. DC and Chrissie looked around them to see where it was coming from. Behind a blackberry bush were Pete and his leaf, caught firmly in the middle of a large cobweb. A spider sat in the corner moving her eight legs.

"She thinks I'm her lunch!" yelled Pete in terror. "Get me out of here !"

DC seized a thorn and swiftly cut Pete and his leaf out of the web. They all hurried away from the bush so quickly that they had gone before the spider realised what was happening. Pete was rather bruised from bumping into a branch so when they were back home again Chrissie put witch-hazel on his head. Then she said briskly, "I think it would be much safer and quieter if all the Butterfly Children helped me to pick the nuts and berries I need."

She gave them each a basket and obediently they spent the afternoon collecting fruit and nuts until the evening, when the damp, chilly mists sent them scurrying to their flowers to sleep and dream of the glowing colours and roaring winds of autumn.